Korky Paul and Valerie Thomas

Winnie in Winter

Winnie the Witch looked out of her
window and shivered.
Her garden was covered in snow.
Her pond was covered in ice.
Icicles hung from the roof tops.
'I'm tired of winter,' said Winnie.

Wilbur came in through the cat flap.
His feet were wet, and his whiskers
were frozen.
Wilbur was tired of winter, too.

Suddenly, Winnie had an idea.

She stopped what she was doing, took down her big book of spells, and read it carefully.

Then she put on her woolly coat, her fluffy hat,
her snow boots, her gloves, and her scarf.
She picked up her wand and she went outside.

Wilbur already had a fur coat on, so he went
outside too. He thought something exciting
might happen, and he wanted to watch.

Winnie shut her eyes.
Then she stood on tiptoe, counted to ten,
waved her wand five times, and shouted,

ABRACADABRA!

And something magical happened!

Above Winnie's house the sun shone brightly.
The sky was deep blue.
All the snow had disappeared.
It was no longer winter at Winnie's house.
It was sunny summer.

Winnie took off her woolly coat, her fluffy hat,
her snow boots, her gloves, and her scarf.
She got her deck chair and went out in the
garden to sit in the sun.
'This is lovely,' said Winnie.
'Summer is much nicer.'

Wilbur lay down in the sun and purred.
This is lovely, he thought.
Summer is much nicer than winter.

All over the garden, little animals were waking up.
They had been having their winter sleep, and they
were very cross.

They came out into the garden, yawning sleepily.
'It's too early for summer,' they grumbled.
'We want to go back to sleep.'

The flowers had been asleep under the snow.
They woke up and began to grow.
Up came the leaves, and then the flowers.

But the sun was too hot for them.
Their heads began to droop.
All the lovely flowers were dying.

Winnie was worried.
The animals and the flowers didn't like
her lovely summer.

Then she heard a very strange noise . . .

Winnie turned around, and there behind her
was a great crowd of people.
They were running along the road towards her house.

They crowded into her garden.
They took off their coats, their hats,
their boots, their gloves,
and their scarves.

Then they sat in the sunshine.
They walked on Winnie's flowers.
They put orange peel on Winnie's grass.
They paddled in Winnie's pond.

Soon there was no room for Winnie
and Wilbur in the garden.
They went inside and looked out
of the window.
The noise was horrible.
The mess was horrible.
Winnie's lovely summer was horrible.

Then Winnie heard another strange noise.
A tinkling noise . . .

Somebody was selling ice creams in her garden.

Winnie was furious.
She grabbed her wand.
She rushed outside.
She stamped her foot, shut her eyes,
counted to ten, waved her wand five times
and shouted,

ABRACADABRA!

The sun disappeared.
The blue sky disappeared.
And the snow began to fall.

The people put on their coats, their hats, their boots, their gloves, and their scarves, and rushed home.
The animals went back to bed, to finish their winter sleep.
The flowers went back under the ground to wait for spring.

Winnie and Wilbur went back inside.
Winnie made a cup of hot chocolate
and toasted a muffin.
Wilbur had a saucer of warm milk.

Then Winnie snuggled into bed.
Wilbur curled up at the foot of
the bed and purred.
'This is warm and cosy,' said Winnie.
'Winter is lovely too.'